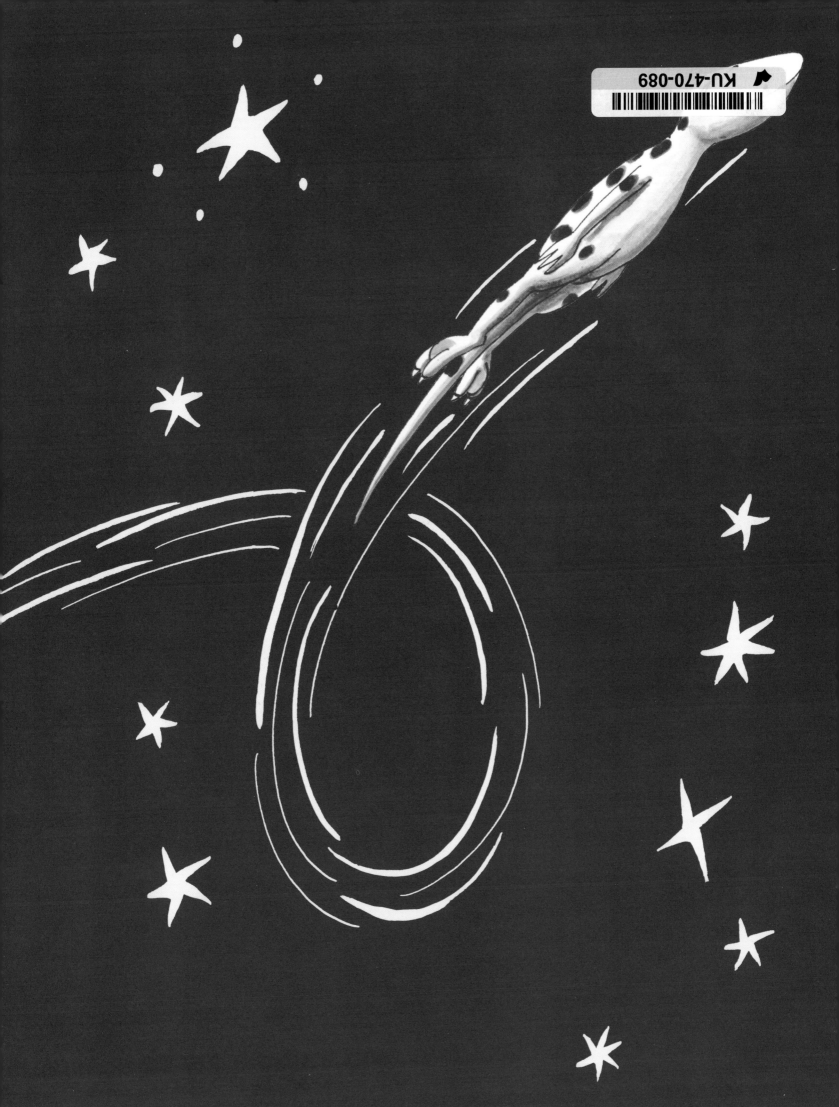

Bumpus Jumpus
Dinosaurumpus!

For Maud, Milly and Ben – T.M.

For Sarah, with love – G.P-R.

Orchard Books
96 Leonard Street, London EC2A 4XD
Orchard Books Australia
Unit 31/56 O'Riordan Street, Alexandria, NSW 2015
This edition produced for The Book People Ltd
Hall Wood Avenue, Haydock, St Helens WA11 9UL
ISBN 1 84362 190 8
Text © Tony Mitton 2002
Illustrations © Guy Parker-Rees 2002
The rights of Tony Mitton to be identified as the author and Guy Parker-Rees
to be identified as the illustrator have been asserted by them in
accordance with the Copyright, Designs and Patents Act, 1988.
A CIP catalogue record for this book is available from the British Library
10 9 8 7 6 5 4 3 2 1
Printed in Hong Kong/China

Bumpus Jumpus Dinosaurumpus!

Tony Mitton

Guy Parker-Rees

TED SMART

There's a quake and a quiver
and a rumbling around.

It makes you shiver.
It's a thundery sound.

"Shake, shake, shudder"...
near the sludgy old swamp.
The dinosaurs are coming.
Get ready to romp.

Donk!

Donk!

Donk!

Here's **Triceratops** jumping UP and DOWN doing dinosaur hops.

He wears three horns
on his **big**, **bony** head,

and blunders along with a
Bomp! Bomp! tread.

"Shake, shake, shudder"...
near the sludgy old swamp.
The dinosaurs are coming.
Get ready to romp.

Watch out for **Deinosuchus** with her **snip-snap** grin, as she perches on her tail and **twizzles** in a spin.

Brontosaurus stops for a slushy, mushy snack. His tail starts swinging with a

Thwack! Thwack! Thwack!

"Shake, shake, shudder"... near the sludgy old swamp. The dinosaurs are coming. Get ready to romp.

Stegosaurus stomps along
with lots of her mates.

Clatter! Clatter! Clatter!

go their bony
back plates.

"Shake, shake, shudder"...
near the sludgy old swamp.
The dinosaurs are coming.
Get ready to romp.

Styracosaurus shakes
his collar and his spikes.
Rattle! Rattle! Rattle!
is the noise that he likes!

A pack of **Deinonychuses**
go running by fast
with a **Zoom! Zoom! Zoom!**
so they won't be the last.

"Shake, shake, shudder"...
near the sludgy old swamp.
The dinosaurs are coming.
Get ready to romp.

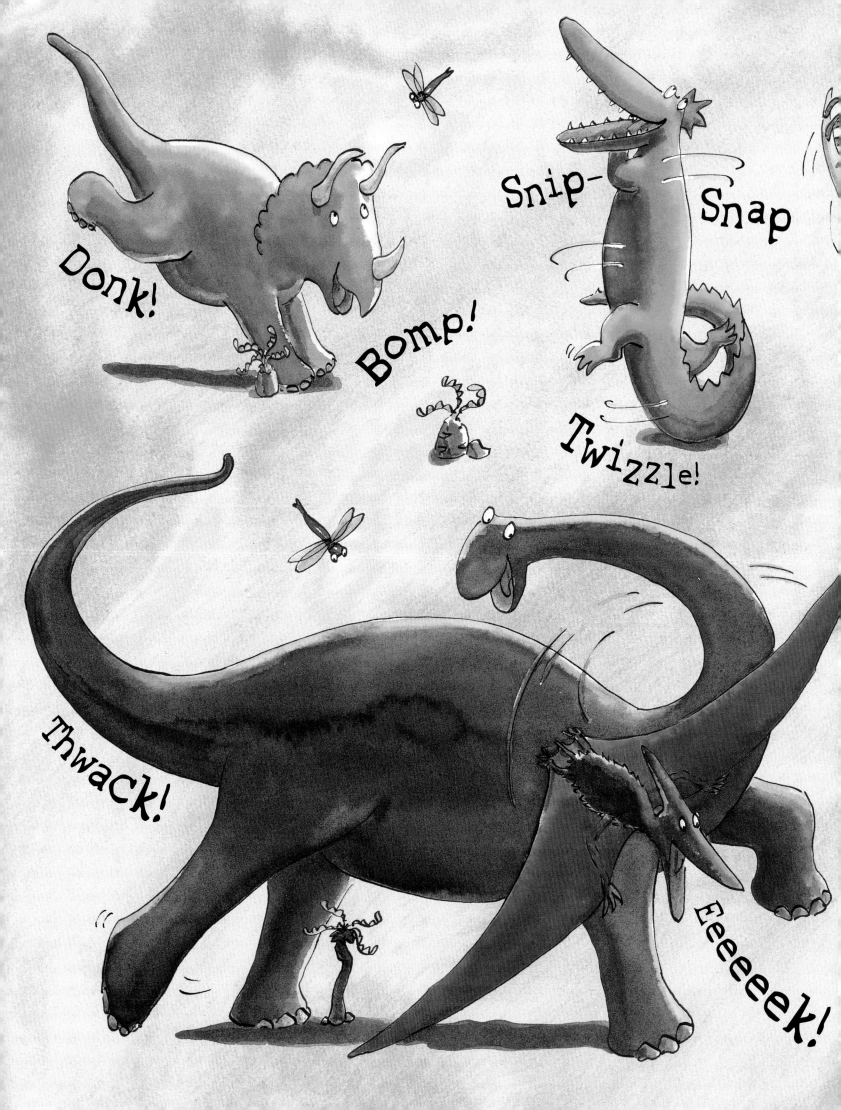

Clatter!

Rattle!

Zoom! Zoom!

Come and take a peek...

"Shake, shake, shudder...
near the sludgy old swamp.
Everybody's doing the
dinosaur romp.

rrrr....!

Roar! Roar! Roar!
Now we're shivering with fright.
What can make a noise like that
in the night?

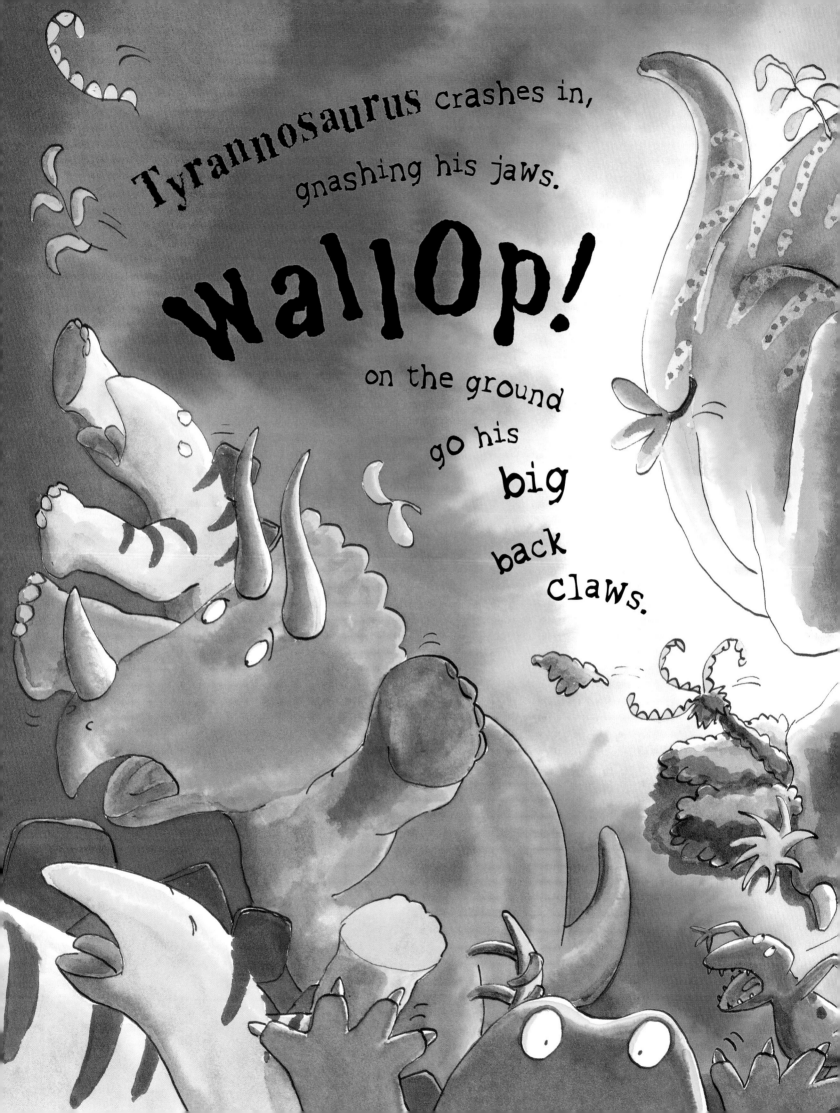

He's huge
and he's heavy,
but all he wants to do...

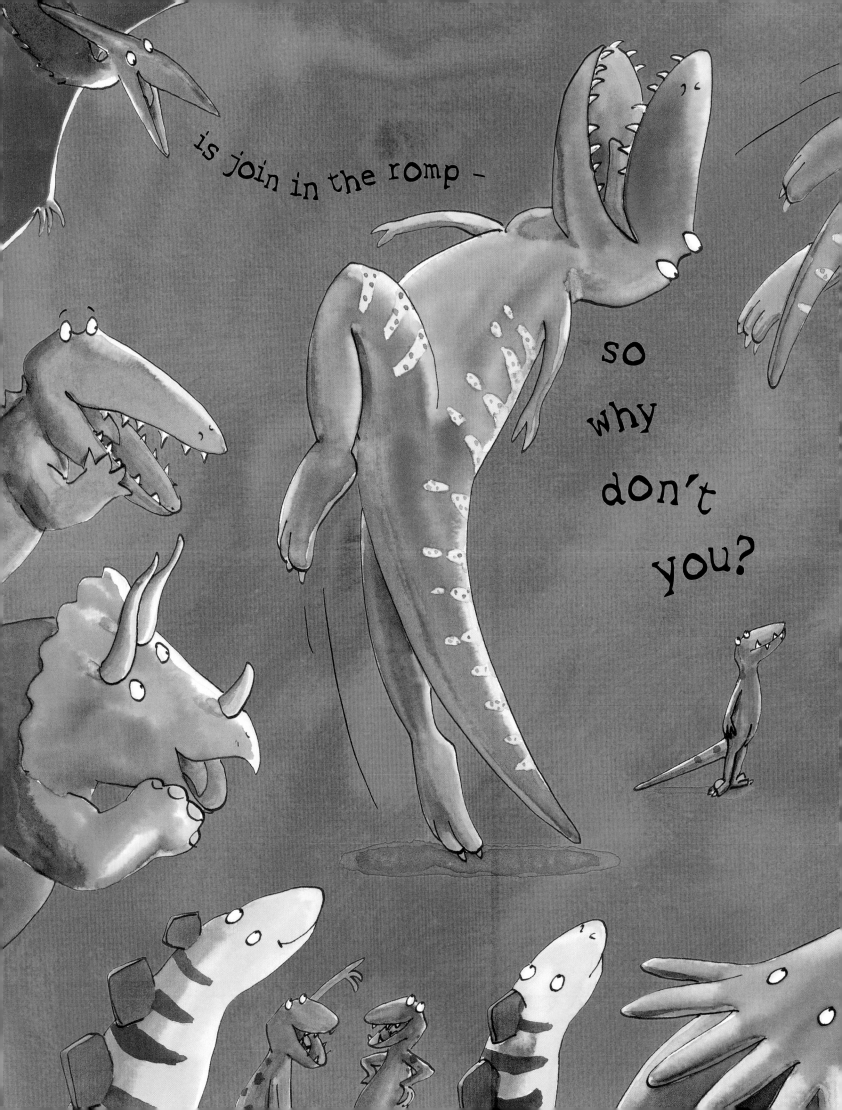

"Shake, shake, shudder"...
near the sludgy old swamp.
Everybody's doing the
dinosaur romp.

Get romping with **T-Rex**
and STOMP! STOMP! STOMP!
Wave your arms madly,

make your feet go **Bomp!**

The dinosaurs won't scratch us,
or bite us, or thump us.
They just want to holler up a...

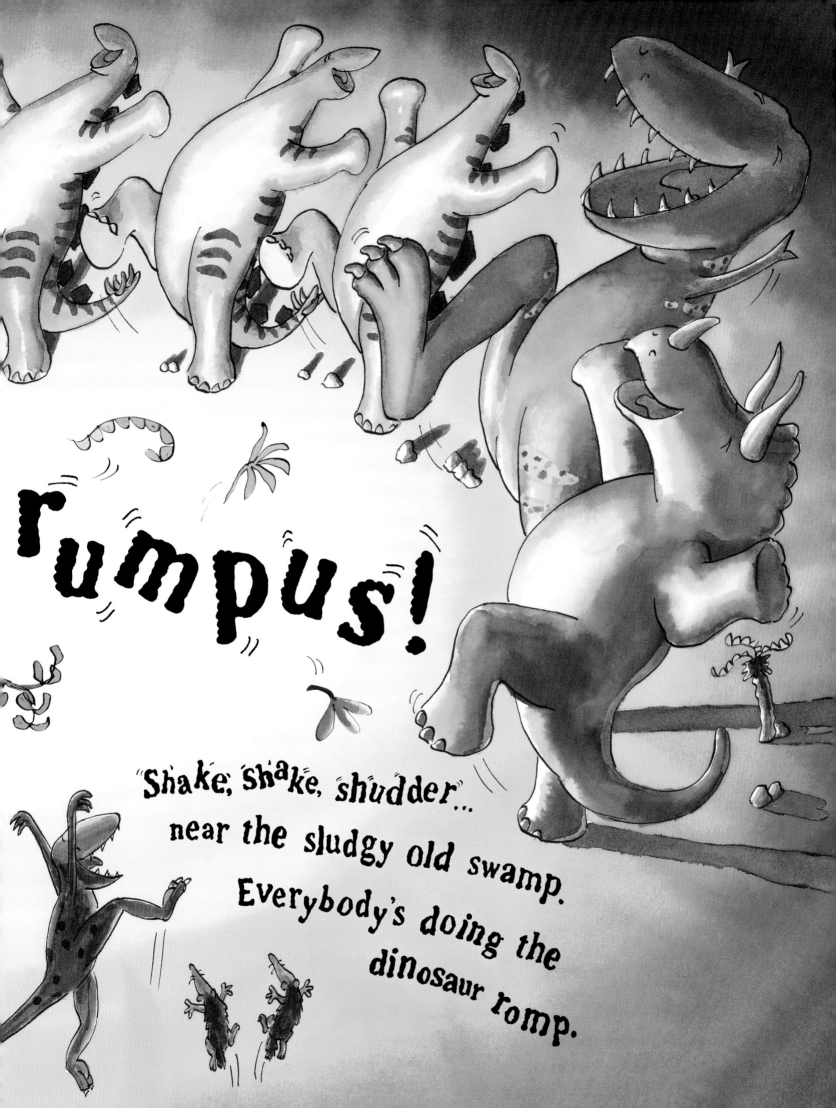

rumpus!

"Shake, shake, shudder...
near the sludgy old swamp.
Everybody's doing the
dinosaur romp.

But soon all the rompers grow sleepy and slow.

The rumpus calms down and the sound drops low.

The rompers drift together
and tumble in a heap...

till finally the dinosaurs
are all fast asleep.

And now the only noise
in the deep of the night
is...

dinosaur-snoring
till the next day's light.